The Urbana Free Library

To renew materials call
217-367-4057

PRESENTED TO

_____

FROM

_____

10-05
$13.00

'TWAS THE NIGHT

THE NATIVITY STORY

MELODY CARLSON

Illustrations by Susan Reagan

BROADMAN & HOLMAN PUBLISHERS   NASHVILLE, TENNESSEE

'Twas the night before Christmas when all through the stable

Not a creature was stirring, though plenty were able.

The ox and the cow and the goat and the sheep

All comfy and cozy, had drifted to sleep.

The morning doves snuggled all warm in their nest,

While chickens and chicks settled down for a rest.

With smell of fresh hay hanging sweet in the air

The critters all slumbered without any care.

Then out in the darkness a star lit the night

Shining so brilliant, so pure, and so bright!

The stable grew lighter as if it were day

'Till the rooster arose, crowing loudly to say:

"Rise 'n shine, everybody!" he cried, "Cock-a-doo!"

The ox and sheep grunted; the cow softly mooed.

And in a few moments, each one was awake,

Confused and bewildered ... was there some mistake?

They squinted and gaped at the glistening star

And then heard a clip-clopping sound from afar.

But after a while the clip-clopping drew close

And right through the door pushed a brown, fuzzy nose.

The animals stared with their mouths open wide

As a man and a woman came right inside.

After heaping the hay to make her a bed,

The man rolled a blanket to pillow her head.

The woman looked weary and tired and worn

Like she had been traveling since earliest morn.

And there in the stable still flooded with light

They settled back down for a long winter's night.

But just as the critters began to drift deep

A startling noise interrupted their sleep!

The woman cried sharply ... like she was in pain!

And all of the critters awakened again.

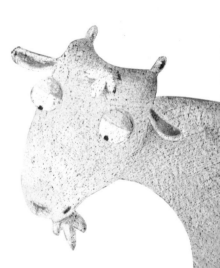

They waited and listened and watched with wide eyes.

Then to their relief they heard baby cries!

So *that* was the problem. It wasn't *real* danger.

The animals smiled at the babe in their manger.

Then just as it seemed the excitement was done,

The animals realized it had only begun!

For in the night sky there arose such a ringing,

With hundreds of angels all joyfully singing:

"Peace on the whole earth and goodwill to us all

For God's only Son has been born in a stall!"

Then down from the hills, the shepherds all poured

To see the sweet baby ... *they called Him the Lord!*

They wept and they worshiped and fell on their knees,

Praying and praising as long as they pleased.

And off in the distance, three learned men smiled,

Then followed the star that would lead to the child.

They'd bring Him great gifts of incredible worth

To give to the King ... to honor His birth.

But back in the stable, the critters were awed

To know that this child was the *true* Son of God!

And so they bowed down, and worshiped the King,

And in their own way, sweet praises did ring.

To Jesus they sang, so real and so right:

"A blessed Christmas to all, and to all a good night!"

And she gave birth to her firstborn, a son.

She wrapped Him in cloths and placed Him in a manger,

because there was no room for them in the inn.

LUKE 2:7 NIV